To Mom and Dad, of course.
And to Sheila Barry. – KL

To John, my favorite. – NN

Published in Canada and the USA in 2018 by Groundwood Books

Groundwood Books / House of Anansi Press
groundwoodbooks.com

We acknowledge the Government of Canada for its financial support of our publishing program.

With the participation of the Government of Canada
Avec la participation du gouvernement du Canada | Canada

Library and Archives Canada Cataloguing in Publication

Lukoff, Kyle, author
A storytelling of ravens / Kyle Lukoff ; Natalie Nelson, illustrator.

Issued in print and electronic formats.
ISBN 978-1-55498-912-6 (hardcover). – ISBN 978-1-55498-913-3 (PDF)

1. Animals – Nomenclature (Popular) – Juvenile literature.
2. Animals – Terminology – Juvenile literature. 3. Vocabulary – Juvenile literature. I. Nelson, Natalie, illustrator II. Title.

QL355.L85 2018 j590.1'4 C2017-905264-0
C2017-905265-9

The illustrations were made from gouache paint, ink drawings, found photographs and digital collage.
Design by Michael Solomon
Printed and bound in China

A Storytelling of Ravens

Kyle Lukoff
Pictures by Natalie Nelson

Groundwood Books
House of Anansi Press
Toronto Berkeley

The nuisance of cats blamed it on the dog.

The memory of elephants knew
the peanut field had to be
around here somewhere.

PECANS
PEANUTS
SUNFLOWERS
ALMONDS

The smack of jellyfish had never
seen a glass-bottomed boat before.

The shrewdness of apes loved the new arrangement. Now everyone would get a snack.

The trip of sheep looked away in embarrassment. Philomena never could keep her footing.

The knot of toads didn't know what to do. Everyone wanted the fly, but not that badly.

The tower of giraffes didn't know
where this new tree had come from,
but it was delicious.

The bloat of hippopotamuses raced up the river. Five words: explosion at the cupcake factory.

The storytelling of ravens waited impatiently for Franklin to finish. They had heard about the big storm of '78 fifteen times already.

The sloth of bears didn't want to forage anymore. Let the food come to them for a change.

The ostentation of peacocks
suspected an intruder in their midst.

The business of ferrets had an important deal to discuss, if Gerald would just finish up at the water cooler.

The parliament of owls expected the bill to pass unanimously, but there was one lone hoot of dissent.

The exaltation of larks cheered. The Hollow Bones was their favorite band.

The parliament of owls expected the bill to pass unanimously, but there was one lone hoot of dissent.

The exaltation of larks cheered.
The Hollow Bones was their
favorite band.